ROBROY
LIBRARY

No. 15

THE SECRET OF ELLEN'S ISLE

"The disguised Prince went first up the rope ladder, but, hampered as he was by unfamiliar clothes, made a most laborious ascent."

THE SECRET OF ELLEN'S ISLE

By ANGUS MACLEAN.

CHAPTER I.

THE ENCOUNTER.

"HIST! Some one approaches. Draw back into the shadow."

The speaker, a tall, powerful man, dressed in leathern doublet and hose, pulled his companion, a stately looking woman, by the sleeve.

"Quick," he said, "for discovery means death."

The two quickly darted behind some boulders that lined the valley. Darkness was setting in over Loch Katrine, but there was light sufficient to enable the new comer to see the strangely-matched pair run to their place of hiding.

"He is coming this way," whispered the man, as the form of a Highlander loomed dimly in the distance.

"What are we to do?" asked the woman. "It is too bad, after all our dangers and difficulties, to be thus run to earth."

"Not so loudly," whispered the man. "Not so loudly. We are not yet run to earth If we are seen, we must attack the man, and dispatch him, for dead men tell no tales."

The woman shuddered. "I suppose it must be so," she said, in weary tones.

On the silent face of the water of Loch Katrine lay Ellen's Isle, showing dimly and ghostlike in the growing darkness. The stranger was evidently making for the water's edge opposite the island.

He had seen the strangers, and wondering at their hasty disappearance, he stopped about the place where he had seen them.

"Ho! there!" he cried. "Who are you, and why do you run from the presence of an honest man?"

Only the echo of his voice broke the solitude of the place. "Don't move," said the man in a whisper to his companion. "Let him move past us, and then we shall attack. Be ready to help me. I shall creep forward, and before he knows, I shall strike him down."

Receiving no answer, the new comer again shouted his challenge, and irritated at not getting a reply, he sprang from the greensward and sprang over the heather. But in doing so, his foot caught in the undergrowth, and he was hurled forward.

Before he could recover, the man and the woman sprang on him, the woman, who was a heavy weight, coolly sitting on his back and preventing him from moving.

"What means this outrage," gasped the fallen Highlander. "You shall have to answer to Rob Roy for this."

"Who are you?" demanded the man.

"Were I on my feet I should soon let you know was the answer.

"Who are you?" again demanded the man.

"Who are you?" demanded the Highlander, ineffectually attempting to throw off his heavy burden."

"It matters not," replied the man through his teeth. "It matters not, but," he added significantly, "it were better that I should know your name before you die."

"Before I die," repeated the Highlander. "Bah, what care I for death, but I tell you to your face you will rue this deed. I am Alastair MacGregor."

"The brother of Rob Roy?" asked the woman.

"The same," replied Alastair MacGregor, "and I would be much obliged by your removing yourself from my back. You may be a fair lady, and an elegant one, but to your charms you have added weight."

The man and the woman whispered together so low that Alastair could not hear the words that passed.

"No, no," exclaimed the man at length, "he must die. We have no proof that he is a MacGregor, and we cannot be too careful in these stirring times. Were the secret to leak out, our last hope is gone."

"He has a red head," said the woman, in a low voice. "He may be who he says."

But Alastair was becoming savage at his ignominious position, and exerting all his strength, almost hurled the burden from his back. The man, however, rushed forward, and kneeling on Alastair's neck, bore him once more to the ground.

In a flash he drew his short hunting knife, and brought it down with terrific force.

The blow would have been a fatal one, but by a deft movement the woman warded off the descending arm, and the dagger found a bloodless sheath in the ground. So much strength had the man put into the blow that when the dagger missed the mark he toppled forward. At the same time the woman had raised herself.

Seizing his opportunity, Alastair, with a superhuman effort flung them both from him; but before he had gained his feet the man was on him, and they both rolled over the heather.

At that moment another stranger rushed on the scene. Dressed in full Highland costume, with his bull-hide targe studded with brass nails flung over his left shoulder, he was a man of most commanding mien.

"What is the meaning of this?" he demanded, as he sprang forward and dragged the man from the Highlander, and shook him as a dog does a rat.

"What is the meaning of this in the territory of Rob Roy?"

"Let go, let go," shouted the man. "No other than Rob Roy could so use such a heavy man as I."

"I am," replied the stranger. "I am Rob Roy, and I demand the meaning of this in my lands."

"One word," muttered the man as he gasped for breath, "one word in your ear, Rob Roy."

The man pulled Rob Roy aside and whispered in his ear.

Roy Roy sprang back, and uttered an involuntary cry of surprise. Calling Alastair to him, Rob Roy in turn whispered, and when Alastair heard he turned sharply, looked at the woman, and muttered some words under his breath.

"They might have said so before," he added in a louder voice, as Rob Roy doffed his feathered bonnet, and said gallantly to the woman, but in a low voice, "Welcome to the MacGregor country."

CHAPTER II.

ON DANGEROUS GROUND.

"Sir Humphrey," said Rob Roy, as he drew him aside, "you should have let me know beforehand."

"It was impossible, Rob Roy," replied the knight in leathern garments. "We made towards your lands, but lost our way. In dread we wandered about, and encountered your brother, whose pardon I now ask."

"It is granted," replied Alastair, "but a word would have been sufficient."

"Never mind that now," interposed Rob Roy; "we must hie at once to Ellen's Isle before it is too dark to see."

Sir Humphrey advanced towards the woman, this time with a reverent gesture, and whispered to her. "We shall follow the MacGregor," he added in louder tones.

Rob Roy and Alastair strode on in front, and reaching the water's edge, pushed aside the thick bushes and brought to view a boat.

Signing to the others to get on board, Rob Roy seized an oar and shot the boat out into the lake. A few minutes' sculling brought them under the shadow of Ellen's Isle.

Springing on shore, Rob Roy led the way through the thick undergrowth.

"We shall be safe here," he said. "Stay here one moment, until I reconnoitre the cottage. We cannot be too careful."

The others waited until Rob Roy went forward in the darkness towards a cottage that stood in the centre of a densely-wooded part of the island.

They had not to wait long.

"Back for your lives as silently as you can," Rob Roy whispered. "Quick to the boat. The cottage is inhabited by some one, and that means mischief."

They quickly re-entered the boat and made for the mainland. "Who's there?" challenged a voice in the darkness.

"Friend," replied Rob Roy, advancing.

"Advance, friend, and give the countersign."

"I know no countersign in my own lands," replied Rob Roy, in a loud voice. "And by the same token I want to know what right you have here."

"By the right of the King."

"A good answer," returned Rob Roy, "but there is another to be consulted, and that is me."

"And who are you?" asked the soldier, for soldier he was, with his bayonet fixed.

"I am Rob Roy, the chieftain of the MacGregors. And who are you?"

"I am the outpost of the Hanoverian Regiment of foot, and I must ask you and your friends to proceed to the examining guard some fifty yards behind here."

Rob Roy felt inclined to pay no attention to the sentry, but on second thoughts he remembered that he would save himself infinite trouble if he obeyed orders for the nonce. Besides, he wished to find out what the meaning of the military incursion into his territory was. He had an idea, but he wished to make certain.

The party passed onwards to the examining guard, where an officer was in command.

"What is the meaning of this?" demanded Rob Roy. "I expect that under some paltry excuse the Government have again taken the opportunity to raid my lands."

"No, MacGregor," answered the officer, who knew Rob Roy. "There is no desire on the part of the Government to harass you, but there is a certain reason why the troops are here."

"And that is?"

"I cannot tell. It is a secret, but as far as I know you will not be disturbed. Whom have we here?" said the officer, as Rob Roy's companions advanced from the darkness into the light of the camp fire.'

"The first is my brother, Alastair," returned Rob Roy. "The second is George Westwood, a cattle dealer from Glasgow, and the third and most important is Elspet, my cook."

The officer laughed heartily, but checked himself. "You don't buy cattle at this time of night," he said. "You will pardon me, but there are a few persons about whom we wish to see. Perhaps this George Westwood may be one of them. Kindly step to the front, George Westwood."

Sir Humphrey stepped to the front, into the light of the camp fire.

The officer burst out laughing.

"Well," he said, "this is the first time I have known a cattle dealer dressed in the leathern garments. George Westwood, I must arrest you in the King's name."

"How so?" demanded Sir Humphrey.

"Ah!" exclaimed the officer, "your accent and your manner confirm my suspicions. You are no cattle dealer. You are my prisoner. In the morning we shall forward you to Edinburgh for further enquiries."

"I am sorry," continued the officer, addressing himself to Rob Roy, "to deprive you of a companion, but in time of war all courtly rules are put aside. For that reason I must make a further call on your generosity."

"In what way?" asked Rob Roy.

"I must borrow your cook," was the unexpected reply. "My fellow officers are famishing. We have not had anything decent to eat for days, and the advent of your cook comes as a blessing."

Although the officer laughed, there was a steely ring in his voice, and Rob Roy did not fail to notice it.

Rob Roy was taken aback by the request of the officer, but he at once said cheerily, "With pleasure, but under this one condition, that she is not to be detained more than one day."

"The condition is just," replied the officer, "and when we have tasted the dainties provided by your cook we shall return her safe and sound."

Rob Roy turned to Elspet, who was standing behind in the shadows.

"Elspet," he said, "you hear what the officer says?"

Elspet bowed awkwardly.

"You had better set to at once, Alastair, who knows something of the culinary art, will give you a hand."

"No, no, no," exclaimed the officer, effusively, "I could not think of it, Rob Roy. It is bad enough detaining your friend and keeping your cook. I really could not think of allowing your brother to help in menial work."

"Elspet has not been well recently," interjected Alastair, "and it is but fair that I should give her a hand."

"No, I cannot have it," replied the officer, adding with sarcasm, "It is the first time I have heard of the brother of a chieftain volunteer for menial duty."

Alastair's face flushed. "I wish for no opinion of yours, sir," he said, sternly. "Be careful, sir, for though you be in the centre of your own men, I shall make you eat your own words at the point of the sword."

The officer was taken aback, and Rob Roy, seeing that trouble was likely to ensue, attempted to calm the storm.

"Be not hasty, Alastair," he said; "Elspet will be able to give a good account of herself, but I honour you for your thoughtfulness towards an old servant of the house."

"Sir," he continued, addressing the officer, "I do not know what you have in your mind, but whatever it is I hope you may be mistaken. I fancy you have done wrong in arresting Westwood."

"I have my own plans," returned the officer, coldly. "I know what I am about."

"I sincerely hope so," replied Rob Roy, checking his rising wrath, "but you may find out that it may be beneficial to you to be civil to the members of our clan."

"Why so?"

"Because you are here on sufferance. Did I care to send out the fiery cross, we should sweep you off the face of the earth."

"I have no desire to quarrel, MacGregor," replied the officer in a milder tone; "if I have said aught wrong, I beg your pardon."

He had no desire to have the MacGregor clan about his ears.

"Nothing remains to be said," replied Rob Roy, "except good-night, and when I return in the morning I hope that Elspet will have given a good account of herself. Come, Alastair, it is time we were home."

CHAPTER III.

The Rescue.

When the brothers cleared the outpost sentry and got beyond earshot, they stopped suddenly.

"This is a nice kettle of fish," said Rob Roy.

"It is," replied Alastair, "and with a little management it need not have occurred."

"But what are we to do in the matter? One thing is certain. I must get Sir Humphrey away from the camp to-night."

"And Elspet?"

"She must come too. If they suspect for one moment the cause is lost."

"Yes," replied Alastair. "That is what I complain about. A little management, a little thoughtfulness on the part of the Prince might give us Highlanders, who are risking our lives for him, a better chance, or at least a chance to assert ourselves in a proper manner."

"You speak truly," replied Rob Roy, "but in the cause of the rightful king we must not take notice of these small details."

"But the risk," exclaimed Alastair. "Have we not given the best of our blood for the cause and yet here you have the one for whom our kith and kin have laid down their lives gallivanting about the country as a woman."

"Not so loud, Alastair," whispered Rob Roy. "The mountains nowadays have ears. If that officer—what's his name——"

"Colonel Dalbeg."

"Well, if Colonel Dalbeg guesses for a moment, and I am not sure he does not, that his Highland cook impressed into service is no other than Prince Charles Stuart, the rightful heir to the throne, the cause is lost."

"What makes you think he suspects?"

"Everything. The man's manner; and what do they want with a cook? Why, they have some splendid cooks amongst their men."

"Then there is only one thing for it."

"And that is to rescue Elspet, and, if possible, Sir Humphrey Tasker."

"How are we to proceed about it."

"We must hurry home and disguise ourselves. No ; we can do better. We must overpower two of the sentries. I shall take one and you the other. Then we shall dress in their clothes."

"Certainly," replied Alastair, "that will be the better way. Sir Humphrey must be a prisoner with the main body of the regiment, while Elspet will be kept with the examining guard until the morning when the discovery is bound to be made."

"Before that time," said Rob Roy, grimly, "many things shall have taken place."

"True," replied Alastair, "we had better commence at once."

"Alastair," whispered Rob Roy, "you can take the man directly in front, while I shall settle the one on the right. The sentries are some fifty paces apart. Use only necessary strength and gag your man."

So saying Rob Roy shook hands with his brother and the next moment they parted, creeping stealthily towards the unsuspecting sentries.

For some hundreds of yards they advanced noiselessly until they could see the shadows of the sentries silhouetted against the flickering camp fires beyond.

Separated by about fifty yards the unsuspecting men stood as the two Highlanders wriggled cautiously on their stomachs through the heather.

Rob Roy was now a few feet from his man, who suddenly started as a twig snapped with slight noise under Rob Roy's weight.

The sentry challenged, but before the echoes of his voice had died away, Rob Roy sprang on him and bore him to the ground. In the next instant he securely gagged the sentry, and before the astonished man could realise it he was stripped of his great coat.

Rob Roy then firmly fastened the man's hands behind him, and also secured his legs.

Running towards the sentry whom Alastair was to tackle, Rob Roy cannoned against his brother.

"Is that you, Alastair ? " he asked, in the darkness.

"Yes," was the reply; "all right. I have fastened my man up safely."

"Come along, then. We shall first make for the main body and see if we cannot rescue Sir Humphrey."

They glided along swiftly until they came to a series of camp fires beside which rows of sleeping figures were lying.

"It is impossible to tell where he is," whispered Rob Roy, as he scanned the hundreds of sleeping men.

"Look far on the right," returned Alastair. "There is a small party by itself."

"You are right, Alastair," replied Rob Roy. "He will be there, if these men be not the headquarter staff, We shall see."

A drowsy sentry looked up as two of his comrades, as he fancied, passed along the lines and threw themselves down on the ground midst the shadows near the smaller party of men. They numbered about twenty, and lay in a circle. In the exact centre was another figure.

Assuring himself that all were asleep, Rob Roy crawled into the circle, and gradually got nearer the central figure.

At last he was within reach, and he gently pulled the man's coat. The man sat up suddenly and stared around him. Rob Roy, pretending to be asleep, saw that the man was Sir Humphrey.

"Hist ! " he whispered, warningly. " Lie down. I am Rob Roy."

Sir Humphrey started, but did as he was told. Lying down quickly he listened as Rob Roy whispered in his ear.

"Watch me as I leave. I am going to wriggle out of the circle by the way I came. You do the same. Then I shall show you the way of escape."

Rob Roy waited for some time, and at last started on his return journey. Inch by inch he wriggled forward and cleared the circle. When he rejoined Alastair he waited.

Slowly Sir Humphrey followed Rob Roy's example. It was a tedious and dangerous undertaking. The least noise meant detection, and detection meant ruin. Fortunately, however, the tired Hanoverians slept like tops.

At last Sir Humphrey cleared the circle and wriggled away, deeper and deeper into the shadows.

"Good so far," whispered Rob Roy. "Sir Humphrey, you must get up, walk rapidly to the right, keeping a sharp look-out for the outpost sentries. When you see them turn again quickly to the right and follow your nose until you come to a man lying on the ground gagged. Wait by him or near him in the heather until we come. We must rescue the Prince.

"Wait," continued Rob Roy, "until Alastair and I get up. We shall walk along the lines as if we are two of the men and under cover of our movement you must do as I have said."

Saying so Rob Roy arose, and followed by Alastair returned by the way they came.

Soon the examining guard behind the line of outposts came in sight. They had a large fire, and by the flickering flames Rob Roy could see the forms of the men on the ground. Many of them were moving.

"They are on the alert," muttered Rob Roy; "but where is their field kitchen?"

"Away on the left," whispered Alastair.

"Can you make the Prince out?" asked Rob Roy. "As yet I cannot."

"We must get nearer," said Alastair.

As the two crept nearer, they saw that although the most of the men were lying down, that a party on the left were sitting up and eating.

Not twenty yards from them was Elspet, gazing moodily at a heterogeneous lot of camp kettles and cooking utensils. There was a strong smell of burnt potatoes.

"The Prince has made a mess of it," laughed Rob Roy, softly.

"At least," returned Alastair, "they are eating his cooking. Loyal Jacobite though I be, I have my doubts."

"There is no time for strategy," said Rob Roy. "Wait here, Alastair, and be ready to back me up at any moment."

Saying so, Rob Roy strode forward and seized a camp kettle as if he were an orderly sent for more food.

Elspet, or the Prince, as the reader knows him to be, looked up and encountered Rob Roy's gaze.

"I am Rob Roy," said the Highlander chieftain. "Follow me as quickly as you can."

Rob Roy led the way towards Alastair. A few curious soldiers looked up as they saw one of the regiment stride along with a camp kettle in his hand, followed by the stalwart female cook.

Despite the singed potatoes, the officers were enjoying their meal.

"By our lady," said one, "this meal is good. I vote we send for the cook and drink her health."

Willing to make any excuse for another bumper, his fellow officers hailed the proposal with delight.

"Send for the cook; send for the cook! She is a handsome Highland wench, and hang me, though she burned the potatoes, it is the first decent meal I have had since I left Edinburgh," cried one.

"Send for the cook! send for the cook!" chorused the others.

But while they were shouting for the cook and no cook came, Rob Roy was leading his royal master to a place of safety. Joining Alastair they passed rapidly onwards, and by good luck encountered Sir Humphrey, who had faithfully followed Rob Roy's directions.

"Come quickly," exclaimed Rob Roy, "for we have but the two rifles of the sentries," and he handed the other rifle to Alastair.

"My brother knows how to make use of it," he said.

At that moment one of the gagged sentries freed himself and shouted in stentorian tones, "The prisoners have escaped! The prisoners have escaped!"

In an instant the camp was in a turmoil. The sleepy men jostled against each other, while the jolly officers, shouting for their cook, were recalled to their sense of duty.

"Quick," said Rob Roy. "Follow me. Keep close. This means an outbreak of war once more. Alastair, we shall send out the fiery cross to-morrow, and gather the clan."

The fugitives pressed forward rapidly.

"I now know that the light we saw in Ellen's Isle was occasioned by some Hanoverian, but as the intruder is not likely to stay, and as I know of another hiding-place on the island, we shall make for there."

As he spoke they heard the thundering of feet behind them.

"They have got the direction," said Sir Humphrey.

"They cannot help doing that," returned Rob Roy, "for this is the only exit at this side from the glen. We shall soon outdo them."

It was as he said. When the men rushed out into the darkness they fell head over heels in the heather, and in the confusion others came pouring after them, mistaking their comrades for enemies. Pandemonium reigned supreme.

Under cover of the noise and confusion Rob Roy skilfully led his party towards Ellen's Isle, and boarding the boat, once more made for the island.

Daylight was just beginning to appear, and the trees stood out like phantom giants as Rob Roy guided the boat under their shadows.

" Wait," he said as he sprang ashore, " until I reconnoitre."

In a few minutes he returned with the news that the light was still to be seen in the window of the hut.

" Alastair," he continued, " we must use the secret of Ellen's Isle."

" It is the only way," replied Alastair " although it will give but poor welcome or comfort to a royal guest."

" Do not study me," said Prince Charles, otherwise Elspet, speaking almost for the first time. " I have drunk the cup of bitterness. Your gallant countrymen have made heroic sacrifices for me and my cause, and in such poor way as I can I desire to show my thankfulness."

" The cause is not yet lost," replied Rob Roy. " The German paupers can always bounce the English nation, but Scotland will ever remain true to the Stuarts, and it is a survival of the fittest."

The Prince bowed. " Lead on, noble MacGregor, for I fain would lay my weary body down to rest."

Landing at the northern side of the island, Rob Roy led the way through the thick woods, and pushing forward through an exceptionally thick belt of broom bushes he came to a clump of tall fir trees growing closely together.

So thick was the foliage and so closely intertwined were the branches that it was impossible even on the brightest day to see the faintest glimmer of daylight above.

Rob Roy looked upwards at the dark mass and whistled shrilly.

In a few seconds there was a rustling above in the branches, and suddenly a rope ladder dangled down to the ground.

Alastair sprang towards it, gave it three smart jerks and began to ascend.

As he disappeared above Rob Roy turned to his companions and bade them mount.

The Prince went first and hampered as he was by unfamiliar clothes, he made a most laborious ascent. When he disappeared Sir Humphrey followed, and Rob Roy brought up the rear.

The rope ladder led far upwards through the leafy branches until near the top an improvised habitation was arrived at.

Above their heads the branches had been cunningly thatched to form a roof, while a substantial flooring had been made of heather twigs, skilfully interwoven with the branches of the closely growing trees. It was a comfortable house in mid-air, impossible of being seen by human eyes below, and providing a good look out towards the surrounding hills.

" Thank you, Roderick," said Rob Roy, courteously, to a fine looking young Highlander, who steadied the rope ladder with his hand and drew it up as soon as Rob Roy had ascended. " My lord," he continued, turning to the Prince, " you are welcome to the last resort of the MacGregors in time of trouble. Now, Ellen's Isle holds a double secret, for the Germans will never dream that the rightful heir to the throne is living in mid-air. You will be able to change your attire for a more suitable dress." And Rob Roy pointed to a walled-off partition, the sides of which were formed by four trees.

CHAPTER IV.

WAR TO THE KNIFE.

" I must find out the intentions of the Hanoverians, and first of all I must look after the safety of my people," said Rob Roy.

" What do you intend doing, noble MacGregor ? " asked the Prince.

" I intend going to the Hanoverian camp, ascertaining what they intend doing, and making my plans in accordance with their designs. There is not the slightest doubt that they had an idea you might make for this quarter to raise men for the coming struggle, and I am not sure they suspected you. However, we shall see. If there is to be war, the MacGregors shall strike the first blow. Let down the ladder, Roderick, and be on the watch, for I may be hard pressed."

Roderick flung the ladder forward in the only open space there was, and before the end had reached the ground Rob Roy commenced to descend.

He whistled shrilly when he reached

the bottom, and the ladder was at once drawn up.

"Now," said Rob Roy, "first to see Mary, my wife, then to the camp."

Crossing in the boat which he concealed amidst the dense willow bushes, Rob Roy made straight for his house where he was welcomed with open arms by his loving spouse.

Rapidly he told her his story, and what he intended to do.

"But you must have something to eat. first," she said. "Besides, why go to the camp at all ? Why trust those Hanoverians ? They are our merciless enemies. The reason they do not attack us now is that they fear the vengeance of the MacGregors. They are far from home, and think to make smooth speeches until they have men enough to wage war on us."

"You speak truly," replied Rob Roy, "but they are also here to provoke a quarrel, so that they may place the blame on us if war does break out."

"Then," replied Mary MacGregor, resolutely, "why not send out the fiery cross at once ? Why not give the clan warning ? Are we once more to face the bayonet without a moment's warning ?"

"You are right. The fiery cross shall be sent out. Call Dougal."

A strapping young Highlander answered the summons.

"Send out the fiery cross," said Rob Roy, nodding significantly.

Going to the inner room Dougal took from a box a cross made roughly of branches of birch-tree, and instantly set out running at full speed towards the villages, holding aloft the emblem.

In every cot every MacGregor capable of bearing arms seized his claymore and targe and hurried to the meeting-place. In half an hour the fighting men of the clan had assembled.

"This is but a precautionary measure," said Rob Roy, as he addressed them. "Wait here under arms, and if I do not return in half an hour you must fall upon the Hanoverian regiment and preserve the motto of the MacGregors— "Follow and spare not !"

A wild cheer burst from the Mac-Gregors. They were anxious once more to meet their foe, and were chagrined at the thought that the Hanoverians could have stolen a march on them during the night. At the same time the Hanoverians were very desirous of keeping peace with the MacGregors. They had a wholesome awe of the terrible claymores of the Red Clan, and had been sent out merely on the chance of tracking down the Stuart Prince whom they had heard had landed on the shores of Scotland and was gathering men to regain the crown that by every right was his.

Rob Roy marched straight for the camp of the Hanoverians and asked for Colonel Dalbeg.

"This is a nice dance you have led us," said Dalbeg, gruffly, as he made his appearance before Rob Roy.

"What do you mean ?" replied Rob Roy, sternly. "Understand once and for all that I have not come to be dictated to. Yesterday you arrested a friend of mine ; you seized my cook, and now you try to insult me."

"You are playing a deep game, Mac-Gregor," said Colonel Dalbeg ; "but, remember, you must keep a civil tongue to me. I have the power !"

"That remains to be seen," replied Rob Roy. "I do not wish to bandy words. I desire to know why you are here, invading a peaceful country."

"It is enough for you to know that it by His Majesty's command," replied Dalbeg, scornfully.

"I am no German," replied Rob Roy. "We in the Highlands have seen evidence of the treachery of your Dutch King William ; we know the rottenness of your Hanoverians, and therefore I demand to to know why you are here ?"

"Treason ! Treason ! Treason !" shouted Dalbeg, excitedly. In a moment he was surrounded by his officers and men.

"This man," he cried, "has been guilty of traitrous words regarding his sovereign !"

"Pardon," replied Roy Roy, "not my sovereign. I have not yet recognised him !"

"Hear him ! Hear the traitor ! Seize him ! Seize him !" shouted Dalbeg.

"I defy you !" shouted Rob Roy, drawing his double-edged claymore. "I defy you. Defend yourself !"

But Colonel Dalbeg had no desire for a hand-to-hand encounter with the redoubtable Rob Roy, so he promptly drew back while his men closed in upon the Highland Chieftain.

"Stand back !" shouted Rob Roy, as his claymore cleared the air. "Stand back !"

"Forward men!" shouted Dalbeg. "Forward!"

But the men hung back. The first man within reach of the claymore was cut to the ground, and as the steel gleamed through the air the others shrank back, afraid.

"I give you warning," cried Rob Roy, "that unless you leave this place within twenty-four hours my clan shall make war on you."

"We have no desire to extirpate your clan," retorted Dalbeg, from his place of safety; "but we must now make a prisoner of you. Forward, men!"

The men made a half-hearted rush forward, and Rob Roy, springing to the front, commenced knocking the men down, in great contempt, with the flat of his sword.

But from the camp behind a shout arose as several companions advanced in fighting order.

Rob Roy laughed scornfully.

"You would think," he exclaimed, "that you were being attacked in force."

As he spoke a fierce cry arose behind him. Well did he know that cry. It was that of the MacGregors on the war-path.

The cry swelled to a long prolonged roar, and as Rob Roy quickly turned his head he could see his fighting men in their red tartan leaping forward to the fray like hounds let loose from the leash.

"Ard Choile! Ard Choile!" shouted Rob Roy, as he waved his sword. "Follow and spare not, Follow and spare not!"

The living wave of the MacGregors surged forward, and nothing could stop the impetuous rush.

The Hanoverians stood for a moment, then throwing down their arms fled in dismay, leaving the MacGregors masters of the field.

"It is now war to the knife," exclaimed Rob Roy, as he rallied his triumphant warriors round him. "It is war to the knife, and that being so you had better help yourselves to what you may find useful in the camp."

CHAPTER V.

A WATER FIGHT.

When the MacGregors returned home Rob Roy again addressed them, and as a precaution ordered them to leave their houses at once, and take to the caves and fastnesses in the hills, carrying with them all their goods and chattels.

The MacGregors did so, and when the three regiments arrived with instructions to extirpate the clan, they found only empty houses.

These they proceeded at once to burn down, and in a few hours the MacGregor village was a burning mass of ruins.

Rob Roy viewed their proceedings from his hiding-place on the tree tops on Ellen's Isle.

"Everything is fair in love and war," he said, "so we must try to give them as hot a reception."

With that in view he lowered himself with the rope ladder, and crossing to the mainland began to reconnoitre.

Hardly had he set his foot on shore than his footsteps were dogged, and he soon found that he was being drawn into a nicely-prepared trap. Away in front he could see a few retreating soldiers; on the right and on the left his keen eye detected the heads of his enemies bobbing up every now and then from the heather as he was being tracked to his doom.

Rob Roy quickly made up his mind. Throwing himself flat on the heather he crawled for several yards downhill until he guessed that he had thrown his trackers off the scent, and rising retraced his steps rapidly towards the lake.

Springing into the boat he pushed off for the island, but just as he did so a loud shout arose.

Looking over his shoulder Rob Roy saw a boat, in which were half-a-dozen soldiers, shoot right across his path.

The men again shouted in triumph. At last they would capture Rob Roy.

"Surrender, MacGregor," shouted the leader.

Rob Roy laughed scornfully.

"Why should I surrender to such as you. As you seem to want a fight on the water, my certie, you shall have it."

The boat with the Hanoverians lay between Rob Roy and the island. Standing on the stern of the boat Rob Roy sculled vigorously, and shot the craft like an arrow straight at his enemies.

So sudden was the movement that the Hanoverians could do nothing else but look on in wonder to see their boat rammed under their very noses. The sharp prow of Rob Roy's boat smashed into the side of the boat, and as the men reeled under the impact, Rob Roy swung his oar in the air.

"That will help you on your way," shouted Rob Roy, as with a mighty swing of the oar he knocked the men helter-skelter, hurling them into the water.

In a second the men were struggling in the water, and grabbing at their sinking boat.

"You richly deserve drowning," said Rob Roy, "but I cannot see men drown before my eyes like kittens. Here," he shouted, "take this boat, row back to the mainland, and dare to follow me at the risk of your lives."

Saying so, Rob Roy jumped into the water, and swam easily to the island.

The unhappy Hanoverians were only too thankful for Rob Roy's gallant action, and when they had clambered on board they gave vent to their feelings in a loud cheer just as Rob Roy, disappearing amongst the trees, waved his hand in response.

Rob Roy's action, however, was to cost him dear, for it gave the Hanoverians an idea that Rob Roy might have a place of retreat on the island. They had always suspected so, and on the present occasion had taken the precaution to occupy the only house on the island.

As soon as the half-drowned men reached shore, the boat was taken possession of by some of their comrades, who at once set off for the island to hunt down the Highland Chieftain.

CHAPTER VI.

ON THE ISLAND.

Colonel Dalbeg had not guessed the secret. Although he was certain in his own mind that "Elspet" was more or less of a suspicious character, he little dreamt that "she" was the very man for whom thousands of troops were scouring the Highlands. Had he known what he really missed, he would have gone beside himself with rage.

With regard to Sir Humphrey, introduced to him as George Westwood, the astute officer had no doubts. His whole appearance proclaimed him a military man, and above all, one of the agents from the Continent to drum up men for the Stuart cause.

It had been rumoured that the heir to the throne had arrived in Scotland, and so close a watch was kept on all strangers that it was necessary for the Prince, known as the old Pretender, to affect the disguise of a woman. It was most degrading to him, but it was the only way, for as yet the clans had not been assembled in his cause, as was the case thirty years later, when his son, "Bonnie Prince Charlie," made a bid for the throne.

Truth to tell the Prince had no heart in the transaction, and he fled the country before the gallant Earl of Mar raised the standard for him in Aberdeenshire.

But to return. Rob Roy knew the danger, and he was troubled in mind whether Ellen's Isle could keep the double secret—the hiding-place and the Prince in hiding.

As he gazed on the face of the placid Loch Katrine he saw on its banks signs of activity.

"Your Majesty," he said, turning to the Prince, who for the time being was dressed in garments suitable to his rank, "your Majesty, our enemies are diligent."

"What are they doing, MacGregor?" he asked.

"They are preparing to take possession of the island, my liege. You will observe they are very busy on the banks of the loch. They have driven, as you see, many cattle to the water's edge, and there they are slaughtering them."

"Yes, I see; but for what reason?"

"For their skins for one thing, and for food for another."

"But why the skins?"

Rob Roy laughed lightly. "It is an old trick of the Campbells. They have no boats to cross over with. They are making some. With stout branches of birch trees they are making the rough frame-work of boats, and they are covering them with the skins of the slaughtered animals."

"But they will not float."

"Oh, yes, my liege, they will. They are making what we call curraghs—light boats with the hairy side of the skins of animals turned inside. They are perfectly waterproof, and you will soon see how they can skim across the water."

It was as Rob Roy said. Under the directions of some of the Campbell clan—always ready to do an injury to anyone, no matter whom, if standing in their way of making money or grabbing land—the Hanoverians were soon in possession of many shallow boats.

In a few hours a whole regiment was landed on Ellen's Isle. Rob Roy's position was desperate. There he had the Prince in his keeping, and though their hiding-place was not likely to be discovered, yet they ran the greatest danger of being starved out. A movement amongst the trees was sufficient to excite suspicion.

The troops poured into the island, and the captives in the trees had an exciting time of it in guessing where and how the men were being placed.

By good fortune none of them bivouacked directly below the dense growth of trees for the simple reason that the undergrowth grew so thickly that camping there was impossible.

The Hanoverians scoured the whole island, but they could find no trace of Rob Roy.

"He must have crossed the island," said Dalbeg, "jumped into the loch, and swam to the other side."

While the Hanoverians were making themselves as comfortable as possible, the fugitives in the trees were talking matters over.

"I do not believe in this method," said the Prince. "I intended returning and claiming my own in a proper fashion."

"Yes, my liege," returned Sir Humphrey, "we all wished that, but it was far better that you should arrive in disguise and find out for yourself the tone and temper of the Scottish people, particularly the Highlanders."

"We have not found out anything we did not know," returned the Prince, "and even disguised as we were, we have been hunted down during the past three weeks' like animals."

"That is true, my liege," replied Sir Humphrey, "but now you know the real facts of the case. You know what men you can rally to your standard."

"I know, I know," said the Prince, ruefully. "The time is not yet ripe."

"The time is ripe," replied Rob Roy, boldly, "and, my liege, you can depend on the MacGregors to their last drop of blood.'

"Would," replied the Prince, "all were like the MacGregors. Once more you have embroiled yourself, and now we are practically prisoners."

"Not at all, my liege ; but it behoves

us just now to exercise caution for your sake."

"For my sake again," moaned the disconsolate Prince. "I never bring anyone anything but sorrow."

"Not so, not so," exclaimed Rob Roy. "Your safety is everything, for without you the cause is lost. Even now I can call down the MacGregors on the Hanoverians and disperse them, and I shall do it when I know you are safe. The first thing to look to is food. To-night I shall descend from here and bring back enough to last us for a few days."

"You must endanger yourself no more," said the Prince. "You already have done too much, noble MacGregor."

"But it is absolutely necessary," returned Rob Roy, "unless we throw up the sponge now, and disclose the secret of Ellen's Isle, and that must not be. No man knows the future, and later on we may have to use this place or we may not."

"Hist !" whispered Alastair, who had been on the watch. "Do not speak so loud. The enemy is moving about somewhere below."

For some minutes they stood and held their breath. Down below they could hear some of the Hanoverians talking and moving about among the bushes. In a short time, however, they moved beyond earshot.

"I have a plan," said Rob Roy, decisively, "and it is this. To-night I shall make for the mainland, and shall assemble the clan. With my picked men I shall attack the island and drive the enemy hence."

"But," said the undecided Prince, "is there no other course ?"

"There is no other course, unless we wish to remain cooped up here for ever like a lot of fowls," replied Rob Roy.

"It is the better plan," ejaculated Sir Humphrey.

"And the only plan," interpolated Alastair. "Rob, I think you ought to allow me to go and rouse the clan."

"No, Alastair, I leave you a more onerous duty, and that is to defend the life of the Prince at all hazards."

"That I will, and it goes without saying," said Alastair.

———

CHAPTER VII.

A PRISONER.

That night, when the Hanoverians settled themselves down to sleep, Rob

Roy cautiously slipped the rope ladder over the platform and allowed it to descend gently through the branches of the trees.

Bidding all good-bye he commenced to descend as noiselessly as he could. He reached the bottom in safety and gave the rope ladder the three customary tugs to show that all was well.

When the ladder was drawn up, he paused for a moment to find his proper direction. Pushing aside the thick bushes, he saw the reflection of the camp-fires through the trees.

Deciding to go straight forward, he forced his way through the under-growth, and when he emerged into an open clearing in the wood, he nearly knocked against a row of piled arms.

At that moment he was seen. The sentry raised a loud shout.

"Rob Roy is here!" he shouted. "Rob Roy is here! Stand to your arms! Stand to your arms!"

In an instant the camp was aroused, and the men rushed pell-mell towards the sentry.

Rob Roy drew his sword. To attempt to spring back among the brushes behind him would have given a clue to the hiding-place, so he stood his ground.

In a moment the men were armed, and had practically surrounded him.

"Surrender, MacGregor!" shouted a voice that Rob Roy instantly recognised as that of Colonel Dalbeg, "surrender MacGregor!"

"Never!" retorted Rob Roy, savagely. "Never. I warn you that the first man that advances shall be cut down!"

"'Tis madness to resist," shouted Dalbeg.

"Then I must indeed be mad," retorted Rob Roy, grimly, "for I shall resist to the bitter end!"

"Forward, men!" shouted Dalbeg, running forward.

"I have no desire to take your life," said Rob Roy, "but I have warned you."

The Hanoverians came forward at a rush. Rob Roy saw that if he stood he would be overpowered by sheer weight of numbers, so he also ran forward.

"Your blood be on your own head!" shouted Rob Roy, as Dalbeg made a thrust at him.

Rob Roy parried the thrust, and as the same time aimed a terrible blow at Dalbeg's head.

But the Colonel was a splendid swords-man. He simply ducked his head while he parried with his sword. The rush of the men behind him, however, carried him off his feet, and Rob Roy seeing his opportunity, launched out his clenched left fist.

The blow was well placed, and of such force that Dalbeg was knocked to the ground, where he lay insensible.

With a sweep of his double-edged claymore, beating down the bayonets of his opponents, Rob Roy hurled the foremost two men to the ground. But the others rushed on. Another two bit the dust. Once more the terrible clay-more gleamed on high, but one man, more daring than the others, heaved his gun at him. It struck Rob Roy on the chest with such force that he staggered back.

Before he could recover himself he was surrounded, and half a dozen men clung so tenaciously to him that he could not use his sword arm.

After a fierce, short struggle Roy Roy was borne to the ground.

"Waste no time," shouted an officer. "Waste no time. You know our orders. Bind him, take him to the mainland without delay."

Rob Roy was securely bound and carried on board a boat. In a few minutes the mainland was reached.

"Waste no time," said the officer. "Get him into the cart without delay. Get him in before the MacGregors are aroused.

Roy Roy was thrust into a covered cart, and the horses started at once.

"At last we have him," said the officer, "and now, you men, be certain that he does not escape. Close the tail-piece of the cart, and do not halt until you have reached Stirling."

The cart jolted along in the darkness, while Rob Roy ruminated on his position. He determined to escape at all costs.

For a long time he tugged at his bonds. Although hurriedly tied, he was well secured, and no effort on his part could unloosen the knots.

At last, after much perseverance, he felt the bonds grow easier, but as his hands were behind his back the stretching of the rope was of little avail.

Then an idea struck him. In the hurry the Hanoverians omitted to remove his skian dhu from the top of his stocking.

Wriggling into position he tried to bring his knees close to his hands, but he found it impossible. After much struggling he gave the idea up.

Then he tried to bring his knees close to his mouth. The first effort was almost successful, and on a second trial he grasped the dirk with his teeth and pulled it out.

Rolling over on his side he grasped the dirk with his fingers, and by pointing it upwards and moving his body backwards and forwards he cut the bonds one by one.

Cautiously he stretched himself and listened. He heard the guards trampling by the side of the cart.

Stretching out his hand he felt that the covering of the cart was made of thick canvas. In an instant his mind was made up.

Feeling with his fingers where the wooden ribs of the roof of the cart were, he judged the distance between them and with one desperate sweep of his right hand rent the covering from top to bottom.

Thrusting his body through the opening, he jumped clear over the heads of the guard, and before they could recover from their astonishment, he was speeding over the heather in the darkness.

The guard raised a terrible hubbub, but it was useless for them to attempt to follow the dauntless Highland Chieftain, and they knew it.

After much discussion, they determined to return to headquarters.

Rob Roy knew every inch of the way, and quickly doubling in his tracks, he made for the mountains.

There in the darkness he whistled shrilly three times like the scream of the curlew. Again he repeated the call, and this time it was answered.

Here and there lights glimmered amongst the hills.

" Who comes ? " challenged a voice in Gaelic.

" Your chief," answered Roy Rob. " Is that you, young Donald ? ",

" It is, my chieftain. What news ? "

" I have escaped from the Hanoverians," replied Rob Roy, advancing to the mouth of the cave where Donald stood. " In the morning, Donald, you will take round the fiery cross. Every man capable of bearing arms will answer to the signal."

" Aye, that they will ! " replied Donald. " We had been wondering what had come of you, for we fully expected to be again led against the Hanoverians."

" And you shall," rejoined Rob Roy. " You shall. To-morrow morning."

" The men are waiting now. We have been waiting a sudden call," said Donald.

" Are they all within call ? "

" Yes, and ready."

" Well, there is no time like the present. Call the men at once."

CHAPTER VIII.

THE ATTACK.

In the silence of the night the MacGregors crept from their caves and marshalled on the hillside.

At the whispered command they moved off noiselessly and marched rapidly to the edge of the loch.

" Fix your targes and claymores on your backs. Pass the word," whispered Rob Roy.

The MacGregors swiftly fixed their targes on their backs, and moving out in single line, they stood by the water's edge.

At the whispered word of command they plunged silently into the loch, and swam towards the island.

The night was pitch dark, and the careless sentries of the Hanoverians little dreamt that the MacGregors were near.

Noiselessly the clansmen approached the island, and as their feet touched ground they unslung their targes and claymores.

Springing to the front, Rob Roy shouted hoarsely, " Follow and spare not ! Follow and spare not ! "

Instantly the camp was on the alert, but the Hanoverians were too late, for the MacGregors swooped down on the rows of piled arms. It was a skilful movement, and at one blow the Hanoverians were disarmed.

" Surrender ! " shouted Rob Roy, rushing up to the commandant's tent, in front of which burned a large camp fire. " Surrender, if you value your lives ; I have captured your guns."

" What is the meaning of this ? " shouted Colonel Dalbeg, rushing in alarm from his tent.

" It means," returned Rob Roy, " that you are my prisoner. Give your men the command to surrender, or, by heaven, I shall give my clansmen the order to cut them down. And, remember the swords of the MacGregors are sharp."

It was an ignominious position to be

in. Colonel Dalbeg bit his lip, but he saw resistance was useless.

"Pass the word to surrender," he said, the tremor in his voice giving evidence of the chagrin he felt.

"It is well," replied Rob Roy. "Muster," he continued in a loud voice, "in the centre of the island."

By the time the prisoners paraded in good order in the centre of the island, daylight began to steal over the hilltops.

Leaving sufficient men to guard the prisoners, Rob Roy hurriedly embarked his men in the skin boats of the Hanoverians, and made for the mainland.

"Clansmen," he said, as they drew up in line on the banks of the loch, "It is almost daylight. On the other side of the mountains is the camp of the other part of the Hanoverian column. In another hour's time it must be ours. Forward."

With the agility of men accustomed to the hills, the MacGregors swarmed up the mountain side, and pausing to form up at the top they swooped down on the Hanoverian camp below.

The Hanoverians, knowing that Rob Roy was a prisoner, but unaware as yet that he had escaped, fondly imagined that they would not be attacked. The wild spectacle of the shouting MacGregors charging headlong on their camp rudely dissipated their dream.

In an instant they flew to arms, but the clansmen swept down on them like a mountain torrent. So impetuous was their charge that the Hanoverians were bodily lifted from their camping-ground, and hurled down the slopes of the tableland on which their camp was pitched.

"Ard Choile ! Ard Choile ! Follow and spare not," shouted Rob Roy, as he led the men. But there was little need of him encouraging his men, for the rout of the enemy was complete.

Taken by surprise, the Hanoverians fled in panic when they saw that resistance was useless, and for miles around nothing was to be seen but their fleeing figures.

The MacGregors continued the pursuit for many miles. "They will not call a halt until they reach Stirling at least. Then they will have a tale to tell," said Rob Roy, panting hard. "Return at once to the camp. Keep whatever is useful ; destroy everything we do not require, and be quick about it."

"Shall we keep the tents ? " asked one of the MacGregors, when they reached the camping-ground.

"Yes," replied Rob Roy, "they will help to make the coming winter more comfortable, particularly as we shall have the enemy at us for some considerable time."

Detailing so many men to convey the spoil to the mountain fastnesses, Rob Roy marched the others on Ellen's Isle.

Embarking on the boats once more, Rob Roy and his men gained the island.

"Ho, Alastair," he said, as he encountered his brother; "How are all above ? "

"Well and strong," replied Alastair.

"No one saw you descend, did they ? " asked Rob Roy, anxiously.

"Not a soul. I would not have descended without the signal being first given, but the Prince insisted as he was burning with anxiety to know the news."

"It was a risky proceeding," returned Rob Roy. "One never knows whose eyes may have seen you, and if the secret is discovered, then farewell to the safety of the Prince."

Proceeding to the centre of the island, Rob Roy addressed Colonel Dalbeg. "Colonel Dalbeg," he said, "I intend marching you and your men out of the country of the MacGregors. We shall escort you to the confines of our territory from which you will be able to make for Stirling or Edinburgh as you may desire."

Colonel Dalbeg bowed.

"I unwillingly concede," he replied. "When do we go.'

"Now," replied Rob Roy "Kindly give your men the order to march."

The Hanoverians were set in motion and embarked on board the boats. When they landed, the MacGregors escorted them by the mountain passes to the confines of the MacGregor territory, and bade them farewell.

"Next time," said Rob Roy, "we shall dispute your advance, no matter on what excuse you come."

"You are playing a bold game, Rob Roy," returned Colonel Dalbeg. "At present you have the advantage. *Our* day will come." Then, lowering his voice, "I know your secret, and that the woman was no other but the Prince."

Rob Roy did not reply, but merely waved his hand.

CHAPTER IX.

OUTLAWED.

The news that the MacGregors were once more on the warpath and that they had routed the troops was received with consternation in the Lowlands.

The authorities in Edinburgh promptly issued a warrant of outlawry, with a price upon Rob Roy's head.

They also fitted up an expedition without delay, and sent it forward with strict orders that Rob Roy was to be captured, dead or alive.

In the meantime, the Prince, pining for the sunny lands of France or Italy, wished to leave the country without waste of time.

"It were better," urged Rob Roy, "to wait for some days or even weeks, until we see what the enemy proposes to do. One thing is certain, they will send an expedition against us, and while we are engaging that expedition then will be your opportunity to escape to the coast."

"That may be so," replied the Prince, "but I have made up my mind to go now."

"So let it be," replied Rob Roy "Shall you try the west coast?"

"No," replied the Prince. "On the west coast we should have very long to wait for a boat, and then the chance of meeting a boat is very small."

"That is true," replied Rob Roy, "but at least there is safety. The road to the east coast is fraught with danger."

"I shall have no delay," exclaimed the Prince, petulantly, "I have been couped up too long already!"

"And your plans, my liege, are——?"

"To make for Leith and join the first boat for France, or anywhere on the Continent."

"Your commands shall be obeyed. It we are to start we had better move now, before all the passes to the lowlands are blocked by soldiers. This way, my liege."

Rob Roy was about to lead the way when he stopped short.

"One word, my liege. To go through the country in military dress will arouse suspicion. You will need to resume your serving woman attire."

The Prince deterred.

"Is it necessary?" he asked.

"It is absolutely necessary," replied Rob Roy. "The moment you are seen in military uniform you will be detected as a person of importance. The woman's dress is necessary."

With unfeigned disgust, the Prince retired to the shelter, and changed his dress to that of a woman's.

"I have had enough of this disgrace," he said as he emerged.

Rob Roy did not speak, but led the way down the rope ladder. Embarking in Rob Roy's boat, they reached the mainland.

"At least within our own borders we are safe," said Rob Roy, "but it is a far cry from Loch Katrine to Leith."

In order to prevent suspicion and avoid observation, Rob Roy took Alastair only with him, Rob Roy going in front some fifty paces, followed by Alastair, while the Prince and Sir . Humphrey brought up the rear 500 yards behind. This was to prevent surprise, or a sudden rush of a concealed enemy.

They journeyed leisurely, for the Prince was not much of a walker, and, hampered as he was with his petticoats, his progress was very slow indeed.

At the end of the first day's journey, they bivouacked for the night, and started off again early next morning. Their progress was again slow.

They had seen no one on their journey, but towards mid-day Rob Roy, who was far in advance and who had just climbed to the top of a range of hills, held up his hand warningly.

The others stopped at once, and Rob Roy beckoned quickly to his brother to advance.

"What's wrong, Rob?" exclaimed Alastair breathlessly, as he flung himself on the heather by Roy's side.

"Look there," said Rob Roy, quickly, "the enemy are advancing in force. Look to the right at that black patch, and look far to the left at that black moving spot, while far away in front is another body of men—of cavalry, as you can see by their quick movement."

"They are sweeping the country!" exclaimed Alastair.

"Yes," replied Rob Roy, thoughtfully. "The flanks are at least six miles apart, and the centre body is to force the pace. Hello!"

The exclamation on the part of Rob Roy was occasioned by the sudden appearance of a body of horsemen at the foot of the hill in front.

"I did not see them," said Rob Roy,

"they have been riding hard under cover of the glen. They are the advance guard, and they are upon us."

"What are we to do about the Prince" asked Alastair, anxiously.

"Retreat is impossible," said Rob Roy. "We ourselves could easily escape but the Prince travels so slowly. We must stand our ground, and fight out."

As he spoke, Rob Roy stood up, and as he did so he was seen by the cavalrymen who raised a loud shout.

"Not so loud, not so loud," he muttered, as the cavalrymen came to a standstill.

"They must advance on foot," said Roy Roy, "for their horses will be completely blown by the time they reach the top."

The cavalrymen stood conversing quickly. They looked about to left and right.

Rob Roy chuckled to himself. "You need not look about," he muttered, "for the only way to the glen is up the face of this hill, and through this narrow cutting which we shall defend to the last. Alastair, give them a taste of your blunderbuss to quicken their wits."

Alastair instantly raised his horse pistol and fired. The distance was too great, however, to hit them, but their horses snorted fiercely as the echoes of the discharge rang out among the hills.

"Ah!" said Rob Roy, as the cavalrymen, with one exception, flung themselves from their horses. "They are going to act."

Alastair sprang to his feet, and with Rob Roy advanced to the cutting in the brow of the hill. Through it the cavalrymen must pass, and it was not broad enough to admit three men abreast.

The cavalrymen advanced, while Rob Roy shouted to them in stentorian tones.

"Go back," he shouted, "to the place from whence you came, or by heaven your bones will bleach on the mountain side."

But the men's orders were peremptory. There was to be no dilly dallying this time, so they continued to advance slowly.

When they came within speaking distance they halted.

"Outlaw," shouted their leader, "know that a price is on your head, dead or alive.

Surrender in the King's name, and it will go better with you."

Rob Roy laughed scornfully.

"There has been a price put on my head so often," he shouted, "that the news does not excite me in the least. It means war to the knife, and as for surrender it would certainly be better for you that I did not resist. Go back, I tell you, and tell your German master that we in the Highlands care not one jot nor one tittle for all the orders he may give. Go back, or your blood be on your own heads."

While he spoke Rob Roy drew his pistol, and fired rapidly, and the next instant a cavalryman flung up his hands and fell backwards.

The men at once fell back when they saw the effect of the shot, and carried their comrade with them.

"Look Rob," exclaimed Alastair, "the parties on the flanks are gaining ground. They see us."

"Yes, and I see their intention. While we are being held up in front they will sweep round and cut us off."

"What shall we do next? Shall we stand?" asked Alastair.

"Load," replied the quick-witted Rob Roy, "load, and then we shall charge on this party in front, before they are reinforced."

The two brothers loaded their pistols rapidly, and with a loud shout charged down the hill on the cavalrymen. They had their backs to the MacGregors, and at the wild shout of the Highlanders they looked behind them. The sight of Rob Roy and his brother was too much for them, and thinking discretion the better part of valour they dropped their comrade, and fled precipitately.

As they disappeared in the glen at the foot of the hill, Rob Roy and Alastair gave them a parting shot, and began to rapidly ascend the hill.

"Wait a minute," exclaimed Rob Roy, as they came upon the body of the cavalryman. "Wait a minute. This poor fellow is not dead."

"Wounded in the shoulder, I should say by the blood," said Alastair.

"Quick," replied Rob Roy, "rip the sleeve of his coat with your dirk."

Alastair did so quickly, and exposed to view a severe wound on the man's upper arm.

"He has fainted," said Rob Roy, "as he quickly bound the man's wound."

"This will help him when he comes round again," said Alastair, as he deposited his whisky flask by the cavalryman's side.

"Come along," exclaimed Rob Roy, as he bounded up the hill. "The Prince and Sir Humphrey will be in a quandary."

"We shall have to retire," continued Rob Roy. "It is a thousand pities we cannot hold this hill, but we should be outflanked if we did."

"What is wrong ? what is wrong ? " exclaimed the Prince in trepidation.

"We are being pursued," replied Rob Roy, "and we must retreat with all speed."

"Where are the enemy ? " asked Sir Humphrey.

"On the flanks and in the front," replied Rob Roy.

"Ah ! " exclaimed Sir Humphrey "that is bad. Their intention, of course, is to outflank us."

"That is so," replied Rob Roy, "to get between us and home."

"What course do you propose ? "

"To retire at once on Ellen's Isle. Tis our only plan. We could strike for the north and baffle our pursuers, but the sufferings would be too great."

"Yes," said the Prince, excitedly, "let us return to Ellen's Isle, I am tired of being hunted about like a wild animal."

Rob Roy looked at him in pity, but said nothing.

Meanwhile, the advance guard of the cavalrymen, unaware that Rob Roy had vacated his coign of vantage, waited until the main body of the centre division came up. Reinforced as they were they plucked up courage and stormed the hills, cheering loudly, when they got to the top no one was there, and no sign of the Highlanders.

CHAPTER X.

THE PURSUIT.

"You must push forward at all hazards," said Rob Roy to Sir Humphrey, "while Alastair and I fight a rearguard fight. We shall hold on to every hill as much as we can. The enemy must concentrate so that we need fear no flank attack. Push forward with all speed. Alastair and I will wait here."

The Prince and Sir Humphrey pressed forward.

"Alastair," said Rob Roy, as the Prince and his escort disappeared along the glen, "we shall lie in ambush here. you take one side, I'll take the other ; when the enemy has entered the gully let drive with both your pistols at close quarters."

The place was an admirable one for an ambush. The valley between the hills narrowed at the passage between two large mountains, the precipitous sides of which, covered with broom and bracken, formed a deep gulley more than a mile in length.

Scrambling up the bush-covered rocks hand over hand, Rob Roy and Alastair climbed upwards until they found a footing on either side that commanded the ravine. Hardly had they done so and concealed themselves than they heard the cheering of the cavalrymen as they charged the hill vacated by the Highlanders.

In breathless suspense they waited the coming of the troops, and just as the head of the column entered the gulley Rob Roy and Alastair discharged both their pistols at the leading men, only twenty yards below.

The ravine echoed and re-echoed as if a hundred guns had been discharged. The effect was instantaneous. Frightened by the noise, and maddened with pain by the stinging small shot, the foremost horses reared on their hind legs, and wheeling about plunged madly amongst the horses in rear, throwing the head of the column into confusion, and stampeding the majority of the chargers behind.

A scene of wild excitement followed. In vain the horsemen attempted to hold their mounts in check, and their shouting added but panic to the frightened creatures.

The open valley beyond was instantly filled with a swaying inextricable mass of men and beasts, and while pandemonium reigned supreme Rob Roy and Alastair slipped from their hiding places and hurried along the ravine. "We shall take up a position at the other end," exclaimed Rob Roy, as they ran along. "There are ledges on both sides, with plenty of big stones, and at least we can hold them at bay until night falls."

Rob Roy waited for an hour or so, when Alastair shouted across the ravine, "They will not attack to-night ; they are too much upset. I don't think they will make another attempt to-day."

Rob Roy thought deeply.

"Perhaps you are right," he sad, after a pause, "that we had better join the Prince and Sir Humphrey. They do not know the country and may have gone astray."

That decided Rob Roy. Listening carefully, he could detect no sign of the enemy, and signing to Alastair, he scrambled down from his place, Alastair following suit.

The two brothers pushed forward, but they saw no sign of their companions.

"I hope they have not missed their way," said Alastair.

"I hope not," replied Rob Roy, doubtfully.

They walked on in silence, and the sun began to sink behind the hills.

"They got a good start," ejaculated Rob Roy, at length.

"If we are to find them to-night," replied Alastair, "it ought to be soon, for the Prince is not a rapid walker."

As they gained an eminence they scanned the surrounding country closely.

"There they are!" exclaimed Rob Roy; "thank heaven they have kept the proper direction."

About a mile in front in the valley below they could make out two figures.

"The Prince seems to be done up," said Alastair.

"Yes," replied Rob Roy, as he fixed his eagle eye on them, "he does. That means that we shall have to bivouack for the night."

"Precious time lost," said Alastair.

"It cannot be helped," replied Rob Roy, "we must make the best of it."

Pressing forward they soon overtook the weary wayfarers. The Prince was too tired to speak.

"How fares the day?" asked Sir Humphrey.

Rob Roy told him. "We ought to press forward without delay," he added.

"It is impossible. It is impossible," moaned the Prince. "I am like to drop with fatigue, and my feet are like two pieces of red-hot iron.

"Then," replied Rob Roy, "we must look out for a safe place to-night."

Rob Roy soon found a suitable position, hidden away among the birch trees, and commanding a good view of the surrounding country at the same time.

Rob Roy unslung his wallet, and took

from it dried deer's flesh, of which they all partook. After the meal it was arranged that Alastair should take first watch up to twelve o'clock, when he would be relieved by Rob Roy.

Alastair kept a sharp look out, but nothing of any importance occurred until about the end of his watch he observed in the distance the reflection of a fire on the clouds.

"The enemy," he muttered, "and not very far away, after all."

Immediately afterwards Rob Roy awoke and took his place. Alastair pointed out the reflection of the fire.

"It is over the shoulder of the neighbouring hill," said Rob Roy, "we must find out what it means. Do you feel sleepy, Alastair?"

"Not a bit," replied Alastair. "I am not going to sleep while there are enemies about. Do you want me to go and investigate."

"No," replied Rob Roy, "I do not, but I should like you to keep a watch while I go and find out what it means. It can hardly be the enemy, for they would know that it might draw down the fire of the clan."

"That thought struck me," said Alastair. "What do you intend doing?"

"Going to see what it means. Keep a sharp look-out. I'm off," said Rob Roy, as he silently made his way through the bushes and cautiously felt his way down hill.

With wary steps Rob Roy approached the adjacent mountain, and on rounding the brow of the hill saw, some fifty yards in front of him, a camp fire. As he scrutinised it closely, he made out a single figure of a man bending down over the fire, and ever and anon the smell of savoury cooking was wafted to his nostrils.

"He is not a Hanoverian," muttered Rob Roy. "I wonder what brings this wanderer in this part of the country."

Creeping nearer the fire Rob Roy saw that the man was dressed in ragged clothes, much after the style of the gaberlunzies, or travelling beggars. He was deeply engaged cooking a piece of venison stuck on the end of a sharp-pointed stick.

"If the Hanoverians are on the look-out," muttered Rob Roy, "they will see this." But then he remembered that the fire was on the wrong side of the hill for them to see it, and not being mountaineers they would be unable to read the language of the clouds.

After careful examination of the surroundings, Rob Roy advanced boldly. The snapping of the dry heather under his feet alarmed the gaberlunzie, who started, looked in Rob Roy's direction, and shouted "Who's there? Beware, I am armed."

At the same time he drew from his voluminous rags a formidable pistol.

"I am a friend," replied Rob Roy, "and have been attracted by your fire. Do you know that the Hanoverians are in the vicinity?"

"No," replied the man; "neither do I care."

The man was literally dressed in rags after the manner of his class—the gaberlunzie or professional travelling beggar. He was tall and powerful, and even his rags did not conceal the panther-like litheness of his limbs as he moved about.

"Are you Rob Roy?" asked the man.

"I am," replied Rob Roy, "and who may you be?"

"'Ragged Robin,' they call me, and the name suits," replied the man, shaking his ragged coat.

Rob Roy laughed. "Never mind that," he said. "But what brings you here."

"The fact is," replied Robin, "that I have lost my way."

"What," exclaimed Rob Roy, incredulously, "a gaberlunzie lose his way."

"I have that," rejoined Robin.

"Where were you making for, then?" asked Rob Roy.

"I thought I would like a jaunt into the Highlands, and then cut across to Glasgow."

"Strange idea," said Rob Roy.

"It is," interrupted Ragged Robin. "What is it that the poet says, 'Searching for pastures new'? That's what I was doing. Besides, I wanted to see the great Rob Roy."

"And you have seen him, what then?"

"I shall have the pleasure of a long conversation with him. But wait a bit, or I'll be cooking this bit of deer too much."

Ragged Robin bent over the fire and turned a large piece of deer's flesh that was frying on a flat piece of metal, supported by huge pieces of wood.

"It smells nice," said Rob Roy, "and I am hungry,"

"You are more than welcome to a share of my modest meal," replied Ragged Robin. "Will you look after the cooking until I unpack a couple of platters from my wallet?"

"With pleasure," said Rob Roy.

"Be very careful," exclaimed Ragged Robin. "It is just at the point when you can spoil it. Keep turning it over."

Willing to oblige, Rob Roy bent over the fire, and turned the broiling meat.

Instantly, as Rob Roy bent down, Ragged Robin's eyes flashed hatred, and seizing a heavy billet of wood, he smote Rob Roy on the head.

The Highland chieftain, stunned by the blow, pitched forward by the side of the fire.

"Now," hissed Ragged Robin through his teeth, "I have you now. Besides the credit of capturing Rob Roy single-handed, I shall rake in the £1,000 for his head. He will make a fine spectacle hanging on the gibbet at Tolbooth or at Stirling."

Saying so, Ragged Robin sprang on Rob Roy. Fortunately for the latter, the blow was a glancing one, otherwise Rob Roy's days would have been numbered. But it was quite sufficient to stun him for the moment, and before he recovered his senses, Ragged Robin had him securely bound.

"Ah ha!" Ragged Robin was saying as he bent over Rob Roy, "I have you now, my bonnie man. Little did I think I could effect my purpose in so short a time."

"And what is your purpose?" asked Rob Roy, as he looked up fearlessly at his captor.

"You will know when my comrades arrive."

"Comrades," echoed Rob Roy, "are you a soldier?"

"There is no use denying it," replied the man; "I am a Hanoverian, and I set out only this night to capture you. I knew you would be attracted by this fire, and somehow I thought I could get the better of your good nature."

"And what is your purpose?"

"To carry you to camp as soon as my comrades arrive."

"Then you have arranged it all beforehand?"

"Oh, yes. I knew I would catch you somehow."

"A lot to be proud of," retorted Rob

Roy ; " but two can play at this game."

" How ? "

" Supposing you take me to Edinburgh, and to please the mob get me hanged or whatever you are to do with me, you have to reckon upon one thing."

" And that is ? "

" The vengeance of the MacGregors."

Ragged Robin, as we shall continue to call him, smiled grimly. " The MacGregors," he said, " will not know in time. By the time you are hanged, we shall have cleared out of the country. Your clansmen will then be baulked of their vengeance."

As he spoke, there was a sound of movement in the heather close by. " Who's there ? " challenged Ragged Robin.

" Friend," replied a voice, and at the same moment a Hanoverian soldier made his appearance. " Any luck ? " he asked.

Ragged Robin pointed downwards with his finger towards Rob Roy.

" Whew ! " whistled the newcomer, " you are a clever man. Is this the real and original Rob Roy ? "

" The very same," replied Ragged Robin with a laugh. " The £1,000 is mine."

The newcomer cast a suspicious glance at Ragged Robin, but he made no comment. He was also a very powerful man, and he seemed chagrined that his comrade should have fallen heir to such a large sum of money.

CHAPTER XI.

A Tight Corner.

Rob Roy lay motionless by the camp fire, while the other two men sat in silence. Ragged Robin was planning what he was going to do with the £1,000 when he got it, and the new comer was also thinking what he might do if he had the money. Why should he not have it ? What was to prevent it ? There were only three men—one bound and a prisoner, the second entitled to £1,000, and the third, full of strength and energy, jealous of his comrade.

But the newcomer was a cunning person. He did not wish to show his full design. So he made himself particularly affable.

" Look here," he said to Ragged Robin, after he had told all the jokes he knew, " I want to say something to you that I don't want the prisoner to hear. Come over here."

" What do you want to say. You might as well say it now. I am too lazy."

The newcomer showed he was nettled.

" It is something I want to tell you."

" In the name of heaven ! " exclaimed Ragged Robin, losing his temper, " why can't you tell it now. What matter though the prisoner is here ? What has he to do with it ? "

" Everything," replied the new comer, testily. " To come to the point, I want to know how much I am getting out of this deal ? "

" What deal ? "

" Why, the thousand pounds. What's my share ? "

" Your share ? " exclaimed Ragged Robin, angrily. " Your share ? What are you talking about ? Did you capture the man ? "

" I am going to give a hand," replied the newcomer, significantly.

" Look here, Sutton," replied Ragged Robin, firmly, " I know you to be the biggest gambler in the regiment, and the biggest make-believe, but you are not going to ride the high horse over me. So stop it."

" Stop it," reiterated Sutton, springing forward. " It is either you or me. If I cannot get half of the reward, then I shall have the lot."

" You shall have none of it," returned Ragged Robin.

" None of it ? " thundered Sutton. " I am going to have the lot."

With these words he sprang on Ragged Robin, but with a well-aimed blow Robin sent him reeling back.

Sutton sprang again to the attack.

" You mean to have the money ? " exclaimed Ragged Robin. " Do you ? Well, you won't ! "

" Won't I ? " shouted Sutton, drawing a knife and making a furious blow at Robin's throat.

" No you won't," growled Ragged Robin, seizing Sutton's arm. For several minutes they swayed backwards and forwards, and ultimately fell in a heap on the heather.

While they were thus struggling, Alastair, who had become anxious at his brother's non-appearance, crept cautiously near the scene. The loud voices, the curses, and the noise of the struggle at once told him that something untoward had happened.

When he came within earshot he did not hesitate a moment, but rushed towards the fire. There he saw the two men struggling, but the first glance showed that Rob Roy was not one of them. A thought flashed across his brain to retire, but the next instant he saw his brother's prostrate form on the ground.

With a savage roar he bounded forward, and with one cut of his dirk severed Rob Roy's bonds. In a moment the Highland chieftain was on his feet.

"Who are they?" asked Alastair quickly.

"A couple of villains," returned Rob Roy, hoarsely.

Alastair did not listen to hear more. Disdaining to draw his sword, he smote the nearest combatant with his right hand. The blow caught the man on the jaw and lifted him off his feet. Before he reached the ground Alastair struck out with his left hand, straight from the shoulder, and floored the second man.

Both sat up in consternation, rubbing their injured heads, and stared in dismay when they saw Rob Roy and Alastair standing over them.

"Neither of you," said Rob Roy, pleasantly, "will get the money, for my time is not yet come. Answer me, if you had me in the position I have you what would you do?"

"Take care that your tongue would carry no stories," replied Robin, boldly.

"Well said," replied Rob Roy; "you certainly speak out as you certainly deserve death. But I am not to take your lives. Alastair, bind them back to back."

Alastair quickly took the cords that had bound Rob Roy, and securely bound the hands of the prisoners behind them, after which he tied their legs together, and finally bound them back to back.

The bonds were arranged so ingeniously with a loop round each of their necks that it was impossible for them to move without choking themselves.

"Come," said Rob Roy, as he looked down on the captives, "let us go. We have no time to lose."

CHAPTER XII.

A NEAR SHAVE.

Rob Roy and Alastair hurried back to their own hiding-place.

"How did you leave them?", asked Rob Roy, as they hurried forward.

"They were all right. I awoke Sir Humphrey before I left. I got so anxious about you. I knew that if all were well you would have sent a signal back. When you did not I determined to investigate. The Prince was asleep when I left."

"Ah," replied Rob Roy, "then he will be fresh for the final rush towards Ellen's Isle."

They pushed forward silently and quickly, when all at once Rob Roy came to a sudden stop.

"Hist! I hear voices," he exclaimed in a hoarse whisper. "Tread lightly."

As they crept near they discovered that the voices came from the direction of their bivouac.

"Never! Never! Never! I surrender when my life has gone."

"It is Sir Humphrey," whispered Rob Roy.

"Don't be foolish," said another voice. "Your case is hopeless, you have been abandoned by Rob Roy, and you are prisoners in my hands. I hope that Elspet, the cook, is well. It has been a long chase, but it has ended as it ought to—in the cause of justice."

"Colonel Dalbeg," whispered Rob Roy; "he must have stumbled on the hiding-place."

"You lie," thundered Sir Humphrey, "Rob Roy has not deserted us."

"It amounts to the same," replied Dalbeg. "He is a prisoner. If he is not at this exact minute he soon will be."

"Another lie," thundered Rob Roy. "Colonel Dalbeg, draw and defend yourself."

Dalbeg wheeled round, as also did his companion. They were evidently taken aback, but Dalbeg was a brave man, and whipped out his sword.

"It is man for man," replied Rob Roy. "I have no wish to take your life, but necessity compels precaution."

"Draw," shouted Alastair to Dalbeg's companion, but the command was unnecessary, for the man had already drawn his sword.

The swordsmen were equally matched,

but the swords of the Hanoverians were but poor weapons against the double-edged claymores of the Highlanders.

With one blow Alastair beat down the guard of his opponent, and disarmed him. Taking the defeated man's sword in his hands, he snapped it over his knee.

"That for your weapons. You might as well fight with darning-needles as with German-made swords."

Meanwhile, the battle between Rob Roy and Dalbeg waxed fast and furious, Dalbeg making up for the deficiency of his weapon by his great skill. But it was an unequal contest. Rob Roy was but waiting his chance, and the chance came. Dalbeg lunged forward, and as he did so Rob Roy feinted, and with a terrible upward cut shivered Dalbeg's sword in atoms.

"It is again my turn," said Rob Roy, saluting. "You are my prisoner."

Colonel Dalbeg bowed. He was at Rob Roy's mercy.

"I shall be more charitable to you than you would have been to me," said Rob Roy. "I shall give you your life on condition that you go straight back to your camp without delay. I give you warning, also, that if you attempt to invade my lands I shall not answer for your safety. Go!"

Colonel Dalbeg bowed and, followed by his companion, disappeared from view in the cold grey light of the morning.

Turning to the Prince and Sir Humphrey, Rob Roy rapidly sketched his adventures of the night.

"It is time we were moving on Ellen's Isle," he said, "for the Hanoverians are determined to have us this time. However, in the secret of Ellen's Isle we are safe."

CHAPTER XIII.

BACK TO THE ISLAND.

Rob Roy and his companions made all haste back to Ellen's Isle, where they arrived in safety. Giving the secret signal Rob Roy looked upwards, and immediately a rope ladder dangled downwards.

"Donald is at his post," said Rob Roy.

In a few minutes the fugitives were once more safely ensconced in the habitation among the trees, and were looking from the platform across the rippling face of Loch Katrine.

"Whew!" whistled Rob Roy. "They have taken up the chase in earnest." As he spoke he pointed to the further end of the loch where hundreds of Hanoverians were seen making their appearance from the surrounding hills.

Without hesitation they marched along the banks of the water until they came opposite Ellen's Isle.

"Fool that I was to spare his life," exclaimed Rob Roy, as he strained his eyes towards the distant shore and discerned Colonel Dalbeg in front. "He seems to be acting as guide. Is it possible that he has discovered aught of the secret?"

While he spoke the Hanoverians formed up opposite the island, and unloaded many skin boats from their transport carts.

"They are making for the island," exclaimed the Prince, excitedly.

"It is natural," replied Rob Roy, "for they are comparatively safe from attack on the island."

In a few minutes the Hanoverians were under weigh, and poured into the island.

"It is all right," said Rob Roy, quietly, in an attempt to calm the Prince's fears. "They do not know the secret."

Soon the Hanoverians plunged into the wood, and to the dismay of the fugitives they began to collect in the thicket directly below them.

"Rob Roy," shouted Colonel Dalbeg, "I know your secret. I know that the disguised woman is the Stuart Prince. Surrender!"

The Prince was about to reply, when Rob Roy beckoned him to be silent.

"I know you are there, Rob Roy," again shouted Dalbeg. "When I was on the island last I saw one of your men descend by a rope ladder. The trees are too thick for us to see, and the forest too dark, but all the same I know you have a hiding-place above."

Rob Roy again beckoned all to be silent.

"Once more, Rob Roy," shouted Dalbeg. "Surrender at once. If not it will be worse for you. I shall starve you out."

No answer was given, and Colonel Dalbeg gave orders that the thick belt of trees should be surrounded and watched without ceasing night and day.

Rob Roy whispered to the Prince, and

beckoned him to follow. In the inner recess of the hut on the platform lay a huge flat-bottomed boat capable of holding half a dozen men. It was very broad and ungainly-looking.

"What good is that to us?" whispered the Prince, disconsolately.

"It is every good," replied Rob Roy. "At night we shall push it to the edge of the platform, get into it, and by jerking it will slide down the branches and into the water."

The day passed wearily, and as the night began to fall and the camp fires were lighted, Colonel Dalbeg had an idea.

"Why not try fire," he thought, "and burn these people out. They cannot escape for when they touch ground we shall capture them. Yes, fire is the thing."

Acting on this idea Colonel Dalbeg ordered his men to gather all the wood they could and pile it below the trees. This they did with a right good will, and then set fire to the pile.

The first intimation the fugitives had of this design was a heavy cloud of choking smoke ascending through the branches, followed by a lurid glare.

"It is time to move," said Rob Roy. "Get into the boat."

The Prince boarded the boat, followed by Sir Humphrey, Alastair and Donald.

"Hold tight," shouted Rob Roy, as he pushed the boat to the edge of the platform while the branches bent and swayed under the weight. "Are you ready? Go!"

Giving a vigorous push, Rob Roy at the same time leapt into the boat which was launched into space. For a few thrilling seconds it shot through the air and landed with a loud whack on the water. For an instant the occupants were drenched with water and it looked as if the boat had gone to the bottom.

But not so, for through the wall of foam the boat shot along the surface of the loch.

"Row for your lives!" shouted Rob Roy, seizing an oar.

A roar of baffled rage arose from the Hanoverians on the island. For the moment they were thunderstuck, and and not until they saw the boat skimming along the water did it strike them that their prisoners had escaped.

Colonel Dalbeg was beside himself with rage. He stamped and raved and swore.

"To the boats! To the boats!" he shouted.

But all was in vain, for the skin boats were sorry affairs in comparison to the swift flat-bottomed skiff. Before the Hanoverians could get into their boats Rob Roy and his companions had disembarked on the mainland.

"We have got behind the troops," exclaimed Rob Roy, "now for another bid for freedom."

Leading his companions by secret paths, Rob Roy soon left all pursuit behind, and once clear of the vicinity of the loch he doubled on his tracks and led them westwards.

"It is our only chance. We shall make for Ballachulish. Get a fisherman's boat and chance our luck."

Meanwhile, Colonel Dalbeg urged his men forward.

"They will make eastward!" he exclaimed, as he sprang ashore. "Forward, men!"

The Hanoverians, however, were completely at fault. They advanced rapidly eastwards, but could find no trace of the fugitives.

"Spread yourselves out, men," commanded Colonel Dalbeg, "and search every nook and cranny."

The order was obeyed without avail.

"They have escaped in the darkness," exclaimed Colonel Dalbeg, "but unless they have wings—which they have not—it is impossible for them to have gone further than this. They are hiding in the vicinity."

Ordering his men to bivouac where they stood, Colonel Dalbeg set out to search for himself. But his efforts were in vain, and weary and draggled, he threw himself on the heather to snatch what sleep he could before the rising of the sun.

Through the darkness of the night Rob Roy led his companions over precipitous hills and dangerous mountain paths. Their progress was necessarily slow, for the Prince was no walker, and in the darkness travelling was difficult.

However, the morning saw them among the wild hills in the vicinity of Loch Lydach.

"They cannot follow us here," said Rob Roy, cheeringly. "I wish they would, for we should lead them a pretty dance."

"Have we far to go?" asked the Prince.

"Another day's march will bring us to the coast," replied Rob Roy. "I shall go on in front to Ballachulish, and find out when or where we may expect a boat."

On the following day Rob Roy, in advance, arrived at Ballachulish, and learned that a Dutch boat—a smuggler trading between Holland, England, and Scotland—was expected in a few days.

Hastening back with this intelligence, Rob Roy made arrangements for making his companions as comfortable as possible under the circumstances.

In two days' time the smuggler arrived, and Rob Roy and Alastair bade a long farewell to the Prince and Sir Humphrey.

"Now," said Rob Roy, grimly, to his brother, as they watched the vessel out of sight, "we shall settle affairs with the Hanoverians."

Unimpeded by their late slow-moving companions, the two Highlanders covered the ground with incredible rapidity.

Without a stop they hurried on like a pair of avenging spirits. In the middle of the night they arrived in their own territory.

The secret signal was passed round the clan, and in the dead of the night the MacGregors were mustered in martial array.

"Have you been harassed in my absence?" asked Rob Roy in a low voice.

"No," was the reply. "The Hanoverians have been too busy. They have left the island and, together with those who followed in pursuit of you, have encamped by the banks of the loch."

"They have not troubled you at all, then?"

"No, not in the least."

"'Tis well," said Rob Roy. "My first impulse was to fall upon them and slaughter them, but they are only doing the bidding of their superiors. However, they must not be allowed to remain in this vicinity. I wish to spare them."

The clansmen scowled fiercely, for they had no desire that the enemy should escape. Not so Rob Roy, however. He was resolved that they should be spared.

"Go," he said, after a moment's silence—"go to the woods, every man of you, and cut, each of you, twelve long staves twelve feet long. Give them sharp points at both ends."

For a moment the men hesitated at the unexpected order, but on Rob Roy saying, "Go, and be silent!" they moved rapidly towards the woods.

In another hour the wondering clansmen mustered together once more, every man staggering under a load of twelve staves—in reality, twelve young fir trees pointed at both ends.

Addressing the silent ranks of the MacGregors Rob Roy said, "Clansmen, the foemen are not worthy of our steel, but we shall march on them. You are to advance on their camp, surround it, and spread yourselves out at five paces' distance between each man. You are then to plant your staves slanting towards the camp."

In an instant the men saw the boldness and the ingenuity of the scheme, and silently they crept towards the camp of the unsuspecting Hanoverians.

Quietly they surrounded the camp, and planted their sharp, pointed staves.

When the sun rose the Hanoverians were thunderstruck to see their camp enclosed by a huge wall of sharp pointed staves, like an impenetrable forest of lances.

From that wall there was no escape.

"Colonel Dalbeg!" shouted Rob Roy, in stentorian tones, "you are at my mercy. If you surrender you shall have a passport for you and your men through our territory in safety. If you do not surrender, I shall remove the staves and you can measure weapons with the MacGregors."

Colonel Dalbeg understood the dilemma. Even if he did not surrender, there would be no escape from the double-edged swords of the fierce Mac-Gregors.

"I surrender!" replied Colonel Dalbeg, after a pause.

Unwillingly the MacGregors removed the staves and escorted the Hanoverians across country.

"Farewell, MacGregor," said Colonel Dalbeg. "I thank you."

"Farewell, Colonel Dalbeg," returned Rob Roy. "I hope next time you come as a friend, for now the Prince is out of the country there is no occasion for any secret on Ellen's Isle."

THE END.

Published by JAMES HENDERSON & SONS, at Red Lion House, Red Lion-court, Fleet-street, E.C.

www.ingramcontent.com/pod-product-compliance
Lightning Source LLC
Chambersburg PA
CBHW082054220626
47052CB00006B/1233